The Perfect Potion

Cheryl Davies

This book is dedicated to my mum,
who is as close to 'perfect' as humanly possible!
Thank you for being such a wonderful, kind,
selfless and inspirational woman!

Thank you for being the kind of person
I will always aspire to be. I will be forever grateful!

Published by Find Magic Within in association with Bear With Us Productions

©2021 Cheryl Davies
The right of Cheryl Davies as the author of this work has
been asserted by her in accordance

with the Copyright Designs and Patents Act 1988.

www.findmagicwithin.com
Instagram: @finding.the.magic | Facebook: @cheryldaviesauthor

Cheryl Davies

The Perfect Potion

Illustrated By
Jenny Yevheniia Lisovaya

The cauldron bubbled rapidly,
little Charm sat near and purred,
Luna watched her sister closely,
as the cauldron now was stirred.

Rainbow bubbles popped intensely,
as they jumped from out the pot.
Astrid made sure no ingredient,
was neither missing nor forgot.

Every item measured precisely
and checked again as it went in.
Perfectly the spell was spoken,
so, the magic could begin.
Little Luna watched intently,
as rainbow steam now filled the air.
Astrid made amazing potions,
oh, how she wished she had her flair!

"Maybe I can help you, Astrid?"
Luna desperately called out.
Her request was denied flatly.
"No way! I'm sorry, little sprout!
You know that you're always a jinx
each time you attempt a spell.
Perhaps you could start reading books?
Maybe you will learn to excel!"

Luna sadly asked her sister,
"Can't you play please, Astrid, instead?"
"I'm too busy," Astrid replied,
adding cherries, bright and red!
With such an aching, heavy heart
Luna tearfully slouched away.
Luna could not understand,
why she didn't want to play.

Soon a thought appeared to Luna,
whilst up at the stars she gazed.
"I can make a spell for snow,
Astrid will be so amazed!
We will play together happily,
hundreds of snowballs we'll throw!
Toboggan down the mountainside,
and make witches out of snow."

Luna quickly made her potion.
"I can't wait for all the fun."
Luna really tried her hardest,
nimbly 'round the room she spun!
Spices added delicately,
great attention all along,
Luna determined this time,
nothing in her spell was wrong.

DON'T DISTURB

Luna held her potion tightly,
as she ran to Astrid Gale.
The fabulous, amazing witch,
who was never known to fail!
And with her potion released,
special magic words were cast.
White snow now covered all the ground,
perfect snowflakes floated past.

Astrid shrieked and leapt out the door.
"What an incredible spell!"
But alas, it wasn't what it seemed,
'cause it was not snow that fell.
Instead of snow within the air,
sticky goo now floated down.
When the witches realised,
happy smiles became a frown.

Stickiness was everywhere,
the glue blanket swept the floor.
They found themselves completely stuck,
to the ground outside their door!
"Really, Luna? Not again!
If only you would get things right?"

"I'm really sorry!"
Luna cried,
"As I tried with all my might."

Astrid said some magic words,
which removed the goo away.
She headed back and shouted,
"Don't you bother me! Okay?
I never want to play again,
I don't care if you are sad!"
Luna hoped to please her sister,
but instead, she'd made her mad!

Luna stared out through her window,
and tears trickled down her face,
but she quickly dried her tears,
after having breathing space.
Luna wasn't giving in.
"It's going to be okay!
I will make my sister laugh,
there's still time to save the day!"

So, Luna puzzled long and hard,
how to make her sister happy.
Tickling might do the trick,
but she'd need a hand from flappy.
Flappy was a stunning raven,
feather hues of black and blue.
"Do you have some feathers spare?"
Flappy gladly said, "I do!"

Luna set off to the kitchen,
holding feathers in her hand,
Flappy flew on overhead,
Luna snuck up as she'd planned.
She tickled Astrid everywhere,
and Astrid roared with laughter.
Astrid shouted, "Luna, STOP!"
But could not prevent disaster.

Astrid flailed her arms around,
tickled more than she could bear.
All the potions bottled up,
toppled down upon the pair!
Both the girls now looked around
the total devastation.
All the potions laying spilt,
even Astrid's star creation!

Astrid shrieked, "Just go away!
Leave! I need to set this straight,
I never want to play again,
I'm your sister, not your mate!"
Luna ran off to her room.
"How did everything go wrong?"
Flappy flew off after her,
lovingly he tagged along.

Luna cried out,
"I am hopeless!
I forever seem to fail.
How I wish I could be perfect,
like my sister Astrid Gale."
Luna had one last idea,
to try a spell for perfection!
"This will be the perfect potion,
to gain Astrid Gale's attention."

Luna's perfect potion sparkled,
under light beams from the moon,
Luna scooped some liquid out,
with a magic silver spoon.
But before she sipped the potion,
Luna saw her door ajar.
Astrid then came bursting in,
after watching from afar!

"What's this?" Astrid questioned,
spying magic in the pan.
Taken back now by surprise,
Luna halted in her plan.
"I have made a special potion,
so I can be just like you."
Luna quietly admitted,
pouring back her special brew.

"Oh, Luna,"
Astrid replied,
"I should not have been so mean!
You're a wonderful young witch,
with a heart that should be seen!
You're doing amazing, Luna,
you're a rising witchling star!
Everyone has to get things wrong,
keep on going, you'll go far!"

Luna listened carefully.
"I can be happy being me?"
Luna's sister's words appealed,
she began to feel carefree.
"I'm so sorry that I shouted,
and told you to go away.
Please can you forgive me, Luna?
we can still go out to play!"

Astrid said,
"More than anything, love
and friendship's what I need!
Perfection is not even real."
And at last, they both agreed.
Luna took her untouched potion,
and she poured it all away.
"I don't need the perfect potion,
I'm now happy anyway!"

Astrid took her sister's hand,
and they stepped out in the dark.
They leap-frogged and played broomstick chase,
as they whizzed around the park.
Both had so much fun together,
as the night turned into day.
Hand in hand they flew together
as the sun now shone away.

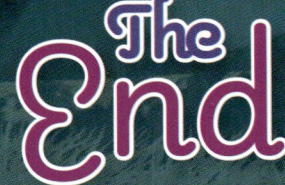
The End

MEET THE WRITER

TAURUS
MUM
WIFE
U.K.

LOVE

MY CHILDREN
FAMILY
MY DOG
HOLIDAYS
EXPLORING
BEING CREATIVE
SUMMER
PICNICS

MOVIES

ALL DISNEY; ROM COM'S;
BIG; KARATE KID;
MRS. DOUBTFIRE; HOME ALONE;
LITTLE RASCALS.

DON'T LIKE

THE DARK
SNAKES
WORMS
CLEANING

www.findmagicwithin.com

@finding.the.magic   @cheryldaviesauthor